Wolf wasn't happy being Wolf.
When he looked in the mirror, he looked bad,
and when he looked bad, he felt bad, and
when he felt bad, he acted bad.

"I wonder whether I have to be this way," said Wolf.
"I wonder whether a leopard can change his spots."

"Of course she can't," said Leopard.
"I was born spotty and you were born bad."
And off she stalked.

Wolf stared at his reflection glumly.
"Actually," said a voice from above,
"it doesn't have to be that way. I often change."

"Oh Chameleon," said Wolf, "that's different. You don't change, you just camouflage."

"That just shows what you know!" said Chameleon huffily. "As a matter of fact, I can change my colour whenever I want. I can be bright when I'm angry and dark when I'm sad. You're not bad, you're just ignorant." And Chameleon darted away.

"Take no notice," said Caterpillar through a mouthful of leaf. "He's just a bit sensitive."

"Caterpillar!" said Wolf. "I know all about you! You get really fat, you go into a cocoon, and then you turn into a butterfly."

"Actually," said Caterpillar, "it's not so simple.
Firstly, only moth caterpillars weave cocoons;
butterfly caterpillars make a shell out of their own
skin. Secondly, in order to turn into a butterfly
I have to dissolve into a mess of goo and build
myself up in a completely different shape."

"My goodness!" said Wolf. "That sounds very difficult."

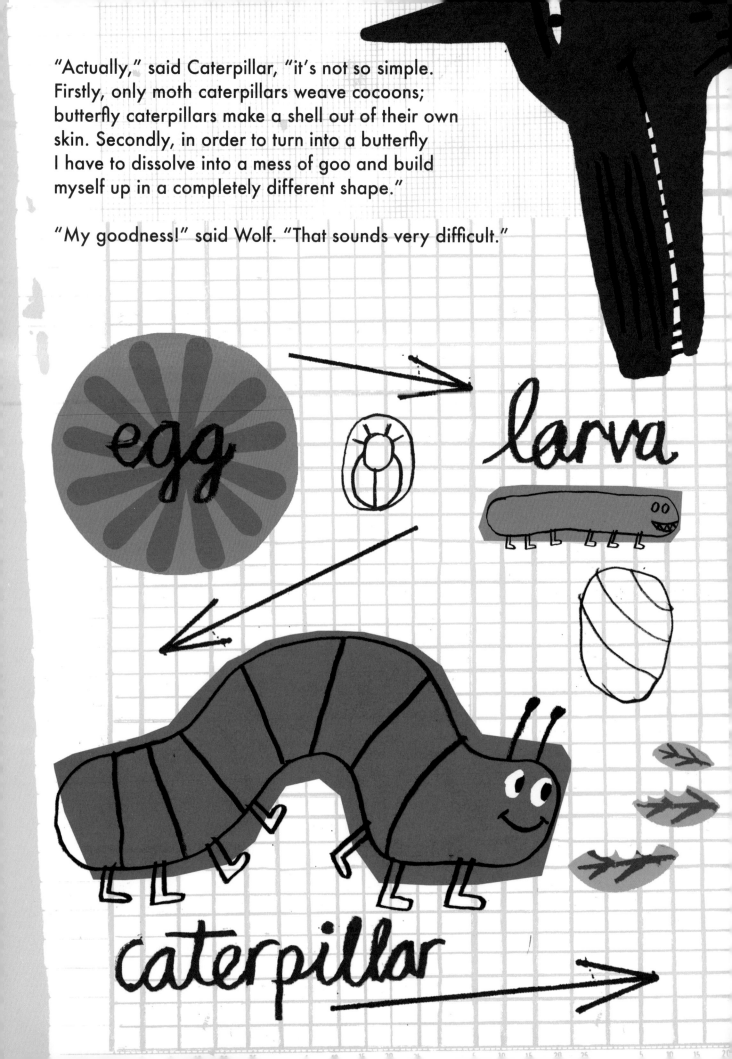

egg

larva

caterpillar

life cycle

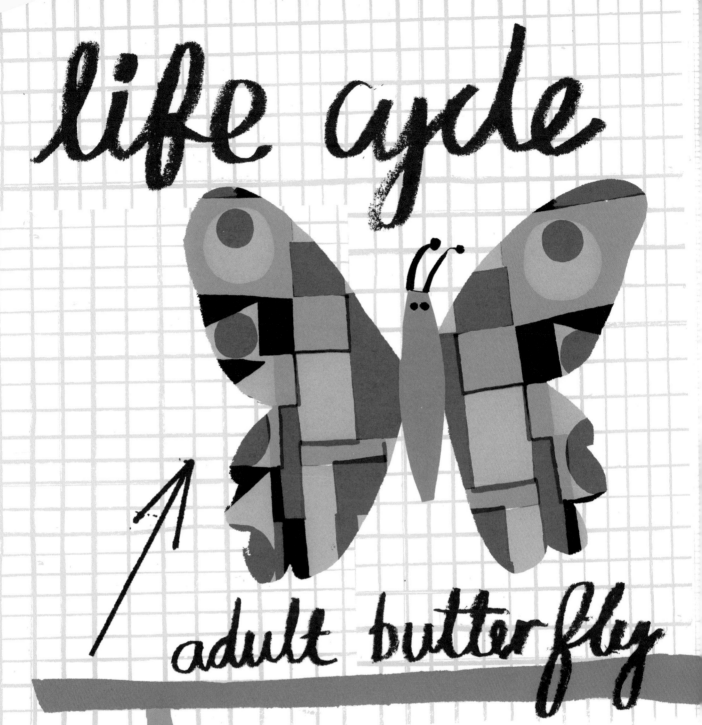

adult butterfly

pupa
(chrysalis)

"It's agony," said Caterpillar.
"And the worst part is, I put in all that
effort and then I die after two weeks."

"Gosh!" said Wolf. "Is it worth it?"

"Is it worth it?" chuckled Caterpillar,
as he inched away to the next juicy leaf.
"Of course it's worth it."

Wolf shook his head.

"I've spent so long being bad I seem to have missed a few things."

"Sounds about right," said Salamander. "Lots of animals change. I bet you'd never have guessed that I once looked like a fish and lived in a pond. Sometimes, to grow up, you have to leave things behind."

She flicked her long tail. "Follow me, I want to introduce you to some friends of mine."

"Everyone, this is Wolf," said Salamander.

"Why don't you tell him
a bit about yourselves?"

HELLO
my name is
Reed
Frog

HELLO
my name is
Mimic
Octopus

HELLO
my name is
Salamander

An octopus floated to the front of the room.
"Hi Wolf, I'm Mimic Octopus. I can take the
shape of five different sea creatures."

At that Mimic seemed to change into a crab,
a rock, a snake and a jellyfish.

"Sometimes it's exhausting," said Mimic.
"I forget who I really am."

"I know that feeling," said Reed Frog.

"I grew up as a girl, and one day
I woke up and I was a boy!
At first I found it very confusing,
but now I'm cool with it."

"Hi Wolf, I'm Flounder," said Flounder. "I know what you're thinking. You're thinking that guy has two eyes on the same side of his head."

"Ummm..." said Wolf.

"Well it wasn't always this way," said Flounder.
"When I was young my mum kept telling me,
'If you spend all your days lying on the ocean floor,
your eyes will move to the top of your head.'
And you know what? She was right. It's embarrassing."

Seal piped up: "I'm pretty happy with the way I turned out. When I was a child, I was snow white with fluffy fur and big eyes. Everyone thought I was so cute, but I never felt I was being taken seriously. I worked hard to build up this thick blubber, and I'm proud of it."

"I don't feel proud of myself," said Wolf.
"I don't like what I see in the mirror.
It's hard to be nice when you just want
to smash things up."

"What would you like to see when you look at yourself?"
asked Seal. Wolf shifted uneasily.

"Everyone's friends in this room," said Salamander.
"We won't judge you."

"Well," said Wolf, "there is something I did once that made
me feel pretty great... but it's embarrassing."

"More embarrassing than your eye moving around to the top of your head?" asked Flounder.

"Maybe not..." said Wolf.

"If it feels right, it probably is right," said Salamander.

"You know what?" said Wolf.
"I'm going to give it a go."

EXIT

"So," said Salamander, "how do you feel?"

I FEEL GOOD!

For Holly & Bonnie

BORN BAD

Illustrated by Stephen Smith
Written by C K Smouha

British Library Cataloguing-in-Publication Data.

A CIP record for this book is available from the British Library.
ISBN: 978-1-908714-75-6

First published by Cicada Books Ltd
48 Burghley Road
London, NW5 1UE
www.cicadabooks.co.uk

© Cicada Books Limited
First paperback edition, 2020

Printed in China

CO

Cicada Books Limited
48 Burghley Road
London NW5 1UE
www.cicadabooks.co.uk